My Guide Inside

Knowing Myself and Understanding My World
(Book II)
Intermediate Teacher's Manual
For Continuation, Intermediate MGI Learner Book

Christa Campsall
with
Kathy Marshall Emerson

3 Principles Ed Talks
myguideinside.com

CCB Publishing
British Columbia, Canada

My Guide Inside (Book II) Intermediate Teacher's Manual

Copyright © 2017, 2020, 2024 by Christa Campsall - http://www.myguideinside.com
My Guide Inside® is a registered trademark of Christa Campsall (3 Principles Ed Talks)
ISBN-13   978-1-77143-591-8
Second Edition

Library and Archives Canada Cataloguing in Publication
Title: My guide inside (book II) intermediate teacher's manual / by Christa Campsall with Kathy Marshall Emerson.
Names: Campsall, Christa, author.
Issued in print and electronic formats.
ISBN 9781771435918 (softcover) | ISBN 9781771435925 (PDF)
Additional cataloguing data available from Library and Archives Canada

Authored with: Kathy Marshall Emerson
Conceptual Development: Barbara Aust and Kathy Marshall Emerson
Design: Josephine Aucoin
Production: Tom Tucker
Contributions: Jane Tucker
Webmaster: Michael Campsall

E-books, MGI Online, Video on Demand Classes, Video Clips, and Digital Media Tools:
See www.**myguideinside.com** for information on these resources.

The author has taken extreme care to ensure that all information in this book is accurate and current at the time of publication. Neither the author nor the publisher can be held responsible for any errors or omissions. Likewise, no liability is assumed for any damage caused by the use of the information from this publication.

All rights reserved. No part of this work may be reproduced in any form – graphically, electronically or mechanically – or processed, duplicated or distributed using electronic systems without the written permission of the author, except for reviewers who may quote brief passages. Any request for photocopying, recording, taping or storage in information systems for any part of this work should be made in writing to the author at: **myguideinside.com**

Why an Owl? Over the years as a classroom teacher, Christa was given various owl gifts. She loves them as symbols of the wisdom we all share. Starting in ancient times and throughout history, various cultures have seen the owl as linked with wisdom and guidance. The owl's big, round eyes symbolize seeing knowledge. Although it is sometimes linked to other ideas, it is because of this connection to wisdom, guidance, and seeing knowledge that the owl was chosen as the graphic symbol for *My Guide Inside (MGI)*. Christa hopes this interpretation is also meaningful to you. One of her former students, Jo Aucoin, now a graphic artist, was commissioned to create the *MGI* owls and clouds graphics.

Publisher: CCB Publishing
              British Columbia, Canada
              www.ccbpublishing.com

My Guide Inside® (Book II) Teacher's Manual

Contents

Promise of Change
    Outcomes: What Intermediate Students Report iv
    Foreword v
    Objectives of *My Guide Inside* vi
    Encouragement to Teachers 1

Overview for Teaching *My Guide Inside* 2

Introduction to Objectives and Lesson Plans 7
    <u>Learning the Foundation</u>
    Lesson Plan Chapter 1 Discovering *My Guide Inside* 8
    Lesson Plan Chapter 2 Knowing The Most Wonderful Gift Ever 10
    <u>Learning from Life</u>
    Lesson Plan Chapter 3 Sharing = Caring 12
    Lesson Plan Chapter 4 Riding the Wave 14
    Lesson Plan Chapter 5 The Best Ship is Friendship 16
    Lesson Plan Chapter 6 What a Difference an Insight Makes 18
    <u>Moving Forward</u>
    Lesson Plan Chapter 7 Wheels of Learning Keep on Turning 20
    Lesson Plan Chapter 8 You are a Wonder 22
    Lesson Plan Chapter 9 Power Words 25

Assessment and Evaluation Rating Scales 26

Integrating My Guide Inside in Education
    Current Education Policy Context 31
    Educational Learning Objectives and Competencies 33

Supplemental Resources
    Recommended Three Principles Resources 35
    Continued Learning for Educators 35
    Websites 37
    MGI in Context of Current Research and Theory 37

  Acknowledgments 41
  Overview of *My Guide Inside* Comprehensive Curriculum 42
    About the Authors 42
    What Professionals Say About *My Guide Inside* 44

My Guide Inside® (Book II) Teacher's Manual

Outcomes: What Intermediate Students Report

Real students, aged 8-12, whom we have been privileged to work with, describe their experiences learning the principles that **My Guide Inside (MGI)** *explores:*

✠ "Knowing there is a power within to help us all out has been the most meaningful thing for me."

✠ "I hadn't thought about 'thought' and it made me think! The way you see life affects life."

✠ "This class has helped me … to not let myself get mad and to have another person have an effect on me to ruin my day."

✠ "I couldn't figure out this problem. So I put it down and then it came to me. If you have a calm mind you can work it out. With a calm mind there is more room to think."

✠ "A thought is like a seed, it grows into a feeling that opens up inside you. Now you decide to let it go, or keep it if it's good, you know. You always have a choice. It's true, for you, and for me!"

✠ "A benefit of optimism is you can do the things you want to do because you know you can."

✠ "Your common sense guides you. I know common sense breaks your negative thoughts. It helps you get on with things and makes it easier."

✠ "It helped me know to calm down when I get mad."

✠ "Almost every single idea or fact I have learned in this class has [helped] me already and will help me."

✠ "The ideas we have shared in class could help not only me but most likely everyone in the world."

My Guide Inside® (Book II) Teacher's Manual

Foreword

Five decades in the schoolhouse showed me, without question, the curriculum and instruction pendulum continually swings from one direction to the other. If you adopt "a new program" students will do well. Wait a few years and something else is touted as the next best solution for improving student achievement and well-being. A decade later, the exact opposite becomes the latest and greatest. If you are around long enough, it comes right back to where it began. This is the lifecycle of curriculum change in schools.

Underlying this continual change is the same heartfelt desire - that educational systems find ways for students to become literate, numerate and function in life as healthy, mentally-well human beings. With the greatest of intentions, curriculum changes from the outside-in are proposed as if we can "open up the student's head and pour in new ideas so things will be different." Use this old "mug and jug" style of teaching and not much changes.

There is another way of educating that is a constant, where innate intelligence a student already possesses is drawn out. *My Guide Inside* is the curriculum that can do just that. Grounded in sound education and resilience research, theory, and practice, the materials have been created to help students recognize their confidence, abilities and their very own guide inside.

Call it intuition, inner intelligence, esteem, personal resilience or any other name that feels comfortable, the essence of it is this: a child learns to draw on their innate capacity to meet with success, to be grounded in mental well-being, to rely on their own judgement. This *KNOWING* lays the foundation for stability in life. It can sometimes seem hidden, but once realized and felt, it can never be lost.

The *My Guide Inside* authors recognize and honor that teachers know their own students best. The curriculum carefully offers suggestions rather than prescriptions. *My Guide Inside* is uniquely designed with "jumping off" points teachers can use to foster important personal learning journeys for their students. I have seen this program in action and have observed the lasting effects that this inside-out way of teaching has.

I encourage you to look carefully at *My Guide Inside* and consider what it can do for your students. Imagine a world where students feel empowered because they *KNOW* they carry their own guide with them at all times.

I wish you all the best in working with the youth of today.

Barb Aust
Retired Teacher, Curriculum Coordinator,
Principal, University Instructor and Author

Objectives of My Guide Inside

This **MGI** curriculum points the way to wholeness, happiness, creativity and well-being in all parts of every student's life.

Therefore, **MGI** has these two academic goals for students: **(1)** Enhance Personal Well-being with an understanding of these principles, and **(2)** Develop competencies in Communication, Thinking, and Personal and Social Responsibility. **MGI** accomplishes both goals by using stories, discussion and various written and creative activities, as the learning increases your students' competency in English Language Arts.

Discovering their **Guide Inside** is key to learning and enhances students' ability to make decisions, navigate life and build healthy relationships. Accessing natural wisdom will affect their well-being, spiritual wellness, personal and social responsibility, and positive personal and cultural identity. Social emotional learning, including self-determination, self-regulation and self-efficacy, are also natural outcomes of greater awareness.

My Guide Inside® (Book II) Teacher's Manual

Encouragement to Teachers

Welcome to a wonderful new experience sharing the principles, commonly called Three Principles, with your students. I have spent my entire teaching career introducing students and educators to these principles. The comments at the beginning and end of **MGI II** are from some of our students and professional colleagues. You can have the same kind of impact! Make the words in *My Guide Inside* come alive and use the teacher notes and lesson plans freely.

As a fellow teacher, I invite you, and indeed strongly encourage you to uncover your own Guide Inside. The words written here, as thoughtfully as they have been prepared for you and your learners, are only an "echo of truth."

Like everyone else in education I also had to find my way. I was a pre-service teacher in 1975 with an up-to-date skill set and a strong desire to help learners who were struggling. Still, I was reconsidering my career choice, because in spite of my desire, I could not reach learners with serious challenges. Try as I might, I could not reach these kids.

What did make the difference? Hearing the truth of these principles. I came to understand the source of natural inner wisdom and well-being; my success rate reaching these learners soared. I had to find "the missing link" for myself, and thus began my lifelong learning journey focused on invigorating the intuitive mind – wisdom – my ***Guide Inside***.

Knowing about this ***Guide Inside*** is valuable for all learners; however, it is particularly vital for struggling learners. They need knowledge and understanding to experience a healthy life. This curriculum is designed for students with activities that can be graded to report on progress; however, it is also for learners who are curious and whose investigation is not based on a need for grades.

As we learn these principles, we find there is no end to the inner wisdom that brings joy and compassion to life. As author Sydney Banks emphasizes, "Those who have found a balance between their intelligence and their innate wisdom are the lucky ones." (1998, p. 133) Let's be included with the lucky ones!

Make the words in ***My Guide Inside*** come alive; your success rate and satisfaction will increase profoundly. Ultimately, you will feel better as you experience a new world. As a colleague who wants to share what works without fail, I urge you to please access the included Recommended Resources and Continued Learning for Educators pages. Please, investigate. These resources are the foundation of ***My Guide Inside***. Happy teaching!

Warmest Regards
Christa Campsall

Overview for Teaching My Guide Inside

As you prepare to share this curriculum with your students, there are some key considerations that can greatly enhance the support you receive from colleagues and administrators in your school system, and the impact you will have on your students. We have learned over the years the following information can be very beneficial.

❖ Curriculum Foundations in Research

Any responsible school curriculum must be built on a solid understanding of current educational research. There are many studies to be considered. (See "***MGI*** in Context of Education Theory and Related Research" in this manual for a discussion and detailed listing of related scholarly publications.) For simplicity we have chosen to highlight the work of John Hattie as one sample body of current significant research.

John Hattie holds a PhD from the University of Toronto and is Professor of Education and Director of the Education Research Institute at the University of Melbourne, Australia. He has also served as education professor, administrator, and research director in various universities in Canada, New Zealand, and the United States. He consults globally with key institutions and organizations. Dr. Hattie undertook the largest ever synthesis of meta-analyses of quantitative measures of the effect of different factors on educational outcomes. Hattie is widely published and most known for his Visible Learning books. His quantitative research methodologies document the influences on student achievement described below.

John Hattie and his team by 2015 studied over 1200 meta analyses related to influences on student achievement. These meta analyses examined more than 65,000 studies, 195,000 effect sizes and about ¼ million students worldwide. Hattie aims to discover what maximizes student learning and achievement (Hattie 2015). To answer this question Hattie identifies the greatest to the least effect size resulting from educational program, policy and innovation interventions.

In general, the *Visible Learning* massive global research story uncovered by John Hattie "argues that when teachers see teaching and learning through the eyes of their students, and when students become their own teachers the outcomes and engagement are maximized." (Hattie, 2015, pp. 79).)

A recent report* with rankings, 1.62 to -.42, indicates these are the top three "effects sizes" impacting student achievement:

#1—Teacher estimates of student achievement 1.62
#2—Collective teacher efficacy 1.57
#3—Self-reported grades 1.33

When seen through a Three Principles lens, educators understand these effects this way:

#1 — "Teacher estimates of student achievement" means an individual teacher's view that each student can achieve/learn; with the educator accurately seeing where a student is at present and then having insights revealing how to move the student forward. As Barb Aust writes, "There are no throw away" students and we reach them by "teaching in the moment." (Aust, 2013, 2016.)

#2 — "Collective teacher efficacy" refers to educators in a school or team thinking—being confident—*they can in fact be successful* in teaching and reaching each and every student. They trust each other to add to the development of a solution.

#3 — "Self-reported grades" indicates the degree to which a student knows that he or she is capable of successful learning which becomes self-fulfilling. When a student learns to drop, "I can't learn" thinking, intrinsic motivation propels the student. It is not surprising this effect ranks so highly.

Additionally, the most negative influence on student achievement is *Student Depression with -.42 effect size*. The impact of student well-being on academic achievement could not be clearer!

What makes a difference? Student's and teacher's thinking plays a critical role. For example, Hattie writes:

"It is less what teachers do in their teaching, but more how they think about their role. It is their mind frames or ways of thinking about teaching and learning that are most critical." (Hattie, 2015, p. 81)

The *My Guide Inside* curriculum directs teachers and learners beyond believing into knowing this is true—that every student can learn and every teacher can discover insights and wisdom to guide effective teaching. Self-efficacy of both student and teacher come naturally when the inside-out nature of life is discovered.

---

* These rankings are visually available at www.visiblelearning.org/nvd3/visualize/hattie-ranking-interactive-2009-2011-2015.html. It is also important to realize as John Hattie's research continues indefinitely, the precise effect rankings and even definitions of effects will vary slightly. For example, in 2016 Jenni Donohoo describes collective teacher efficacy at 1.57 as the most influential effect (Donohoo, p. 6). Despite various interpretations, we feel key identified factors align well with our Three Principles understanding.

❖ **Suggestions for Using *My Guide Inside***

My Guide Inside is based on three fundamental principles, known as Mind, Consciousness and Thought, that are the foundation of all human experience. These Three Principles, realized and articulated by Sydney Banks, offer a hopeful, simple way for children, youth, and adults to gain understanding of how they operate mentally, from the inside out. This maximizes personal well-being, and improves school climate as well as learner behavior and performance.

"Mind + Consciousness + Thought = Reality" (Banks, 2005, p. 42)

This curriculum is most effective when adults who use it are personally familiar with, and living from, these principles and have learned to trust their own guide inside. The common sense of the Three Principles will be natural for students to discover, with the guidance of a principles-based teacher. Every one of us wants to learn and be happy. This is an opportunity for us to also learn from, and with, the students! All instruction aims to measurably impact students and improve their lives. See what kids think: watch the My Guide Inside Overview (5min) and Focus Group Experiences with My Guide Inside video of secondary student outcomes: 5min summary or full 27min interview myguideinside.com.

Intended Use

The *MGI* curriculum comprising story-based lessons is designed for use in a school or home or wherever it is important to bring hope to learners. ***My Guide Inside*** Learner Book II is designed for student success in this context:

Reading Level: "easy to read" (Grade 4-5 level)
Ideal Level: intermediate (age: 9-12; Grades 4-7)
Flexibility: regular course or adapt or modify to suit individual learners
Settings: classroom, small group or individual
Design: inclusive of self-directed learners working independently
Ideal Time: start of a program or school year to build community and foster optimism
Digital Media: Resources at myguideinside.com password: mgi
Videos on Demand for each chapter, free digital media options and video clips

Lesson Time Frame

Each of the chapters will require two sessions of approximately 40 minutes each. This allows time for: reading, discussion, vocabulary building, reflection and journal entry. Any additional activities chosen to accompany the lesson will require more time. A wide variety of engaging activities are offered.

Flexibility and Lessons Plans

The main instructional goal is to have class discussions which foster learner awareness of innate inner wisdom called my *Guide Inside* in this material. We can discover inner wisdom by sharing big picture ideas. This curriculum is meant as a springboard! The chapters can be used in any order that works for you. You may have your own principles stories to share. Your own insights will lead to a deeper understanding. Be flexible. Follow what you know to do.

The lesson plans do not spell out what to include in a lesson; options are fully provided in the *MGI Learner Book* with stories, activities and resources specific to each lesson. Students may be directed to discussion, vocabulary and journals to expand thinking and communication. *MGI* lesson plans do provide details about how each specific chapter lesson can be aligned with student academic progress. The plans suggest how progress will be accomplished and observed as you carry out the actual lessons. This design achieves an opportunity for teachers to be their own evaluator. As John Hattie so strongly encourages us, *"Know thy impact!"*

The lesson plans and the *MGI Learner Book* together offer a way of sharing the principles so that student learning in broad important areas—*MGI* objectives for Personal Well-being Awareness and Responsibility—will be achieved. No exhaustive planning is needed, simply read through the logically organized chapters and proceed. Lessons are easy to use. For specific details see *Introduction to Objectives and Lesson Plans*.

Class sets of *MGI Learner Books* may be used year after year. Alternatively, whenever possible, it is optimal to provide an *MGI Learner Book* for each student to keep and access for further exploration of the key elements.

Video On Demand and Digital Media

Before reading further, please go to the Resources Tab of the website,
     myguideinside.com   Password: mgi
for Video On Demand Classes bring the chapters to life and Digital Media Options for activities.

The website includes appropriate tools for image and banner making, blogging, publishing, mind mapping and video production. These optional Digital Media programs are at the "easy" level of difficulty. Each of these was carefully studied and tested for ease of use. A list of free online resources is provided to support you as a busy educator.

Assessment and Evaluation

All instruction aims to measurably impact students and improve their lives. Three *MGI* forms, with instructions, are provided in *Assessment and Observation*. These tools include: *Learner MGI II Pre- and Post-Assessments, English Language Arts Assessments, Teacher "Snapshot" Learner Observations*. By keeping a copy of each student's Pre- and Post-Assessments, development can be monitored and discussed individually with each learner.

When possible, a school district research office staffer may develop an efficient computerized system for data collection, analysis and reporting to the classroom teacher. Both individual student and full class reports may be developed.

Learning, Living, Sharing

The feeling you bring to your classroom every day, the "essential curriculum," is the greatest resource you have for directly impacting students. In other words, learning allows you to "live the principles" by being in a natural state of service; sharing compassion, understanding and joy in your classroom. Once you are being that informally and naturally, you will be sharing the principles, via a positive feeling. This will enhance and make more powerful any formal sharing you are able to do using lessons with students. Your own deep understanding of these principles will allow you to bring out the best in all students.

I am grateful to my colleague Kathy Marshall Emerson, who has introduced Three Principles to literally hundreds of teachers, for clarifying the simplicity of this process in *Educators Living in the Joy of Gratitude*, particularly in Webinar 12. Also see the very helpful book by Barb Aust, *The Essential Curriculum*, in which she beautifully describes what the school and classroom climate is like when the principles are integrated into educational settings. Barb has experience learning, living, and sharing Three Principles during her entire career; she has always shared such wisdom in her roles as teacher, principal and pre-service teacher supervisor. For continued learning see *Supplemental Resources*. These materials will guide you to your own insights.

My Guide Inside® (Book II) Teacher's Manual

Introduction to Objectives and Lesson Plans

The principles discussed in the **My Guide Inside** comprehensive curriculum operate in all people, including students of every age. The Pre-K-12 **MGI** curriculum points the way to wholeness, happiness, creativity and well-being in all parts of life.

Therefore, all lessons in **MGI** Books I, II, and III share two globally appropriate academic objectives to:

(1) **Enhance Personal Well-being with an understanding of these principles,**
(2) **Develop competencies in Communication, Thinking, and Personal and Social Responsibility.**

Discovering their *Guide Inside* is key to learning and **enhances all students' ability to make decisions, navigate life and build healthy relationships. Accessing natural wisdom will affect well-being, spiritual wellness, personal and social responsibility, and positive personal and cultural identity. Self-determination, self-regulation and self-efficacy are also natural outcomes of greater awareness.**

A guide to *Educational Learning Objectives and Competencies* in all relevant areas is provided below in the section called *Integrating* **My Guide Inside** *in Education*. **MGI** accomplishes its objectives by using age appropriate stories, discussion and various written and creative activities, as it increases competency in English Language Arts and other areas.

Learner Book II lesson plans designed to achieve these objectives with intermediate age students follow.

> *It may be helpful to know*: Each Lesson Plan contains a brief lesson Orientation with the main teaching focus in **bold italics**. Especially see the *Learner Outcomes* placed at the end of each lesson plan. *Lesson Aims and Learning Opportunities* are also included. In all cases, *the first few bulleted items address the chapter's principles lesson*. This may help make lessons targeted and possible to fit in into limited class time. Remaining items detail broader learning.

My Guide Inside® (Book II) Teacher's Manual
Lesson Plan Chapter 1
Discovering *My Guide Inside*

Start with Orientation: Find Your Bearings

Learners are invited on a journey revealing their own natural inner wisdom. They experience their Guide Inside and discover it helps them make decisions and feel secure. With reflection and discussion learners become increasingly aware and find their own words to name their **Guide Inside**. Students explore how their new knowledge grows with them as they experience compassion and joy in living. Trusting inner wisdom "helps you find your balance." The "cloudy" thoughts that cover up a good feeling pass and students experience the "sun" of a nicer thought. Power Words are used in journal entries about wisdom, their **Guide Inside**.

This chapter focuses on each learner's experience and familiarity with their own Guide Inside. Enhanced Personal Well-being Awareness prepares everyone to responsibly know their Guide Inside is available anytime.

Learner Pre-Assessment, found in this manual to copy or at myguideinside.com, is to be completed prior to this first lesson. A Learner Post-Assessment is completed in the last class.

Lesson Aims

Chapter 1 aims for learners to:
- increase understanding of principles with awareness of their **Guide Inside**
- invigorate "knowing myself and understanding my world" through discussion
- enhance language development
- develop reading strategies
- experience creativity with personal writing and art

Learning Opportunities

Chapter 1 is designed to encourage learners to:
- gain an understanding of the principles in terms of
  - exploring the meaning of inner wisdom and naming it
  - experiencing inner wisdom connection through reflection
- develop language through listening, speaking, reading, writing

My Guide Inside® (Book II) Teacher's Manual

Learning Outcomes

At the end of Chapter 1, learners will show skills and knowledge through:
- an understanding of the principles when
    - describing their own experience noticing their Guide Inside
    - using their own words to name their Guide Inside
    - telling a story of how their Guide Inside helped them
- participating by listening
- solving a puzzle by thinking
- communicating creatively and expressively through speaking, writing and art
- discussing and writing about the big picture idea:

My Guide Inside is "powerful knowledge."
Wisdom "will grow with you and guide you."

(Banks, 2004, p. 67)

Resources Tab

myguideinside.com includes Video On Demand Class to bring this chapter to life. Password: mgi

Key Objectives Reminder

Every chapter has two broad learning objectives: Personal Well-being Awareness and Responsibility. With the special focus of Chapter 1, what do the students tell you they have discovered?

Activities

Use Evaluation Rating Scales for art activity, discussion, mural activity, reflective journal entry, and written output.

Special resource

Snow Globe

My Guide Inside® (Book II) Teacher's Manual

Lesson Plan Chapter 2
Knowing the Most Wonderful Gift Ever

Start with Orientation: Find Your Bearings

*Learners discover everyone has the "gift of thought" and the ability to choose which thought to use. Our **Guide Inside**, common sense or wisdom, helps us decide. Thoughts create feelings. We naturally act on thoughts that produce happiness and security. Students try out happy and fearful thoughts. Devan helps his little brother stop scaring himself with bedtime monster and dragon thoughts! It is natural to outgrow ideas as we develop and experience knowing that feelings are created by thoughts. "Opposite Day" and other activities offer a chance to see how thought works. Power Words are used in journal entries about choice.*

This chapter focuses on the "gift of thought" which produces all feelings. Each person has self-determination and a natural self-regulation power to choose and use ideas, or drop a thought like a hot potato! Our Guide Inside helps us make responsible choices that lead to personal well-being.

Lesson Aims

Chapter 2 aims for learners to:
- increase an understanding of principles by discovering
  - thoughts create feelings
  - common sense in seeing choice
  - choice in deciding which thought to use
- gain awareness of self-determination and of natural self-regulation
- invigorate "knowing myself and understanding my world" through discussion
- enhance language development
- develop reading strategies
- experience creativity with personal writing and art

Learning Opportunities

Chapter 2 is designed to encourage learners to:
- gain an understanding of the principles in terms of
  - connecting with inner wisdom
  - experiencing the causal relationship of thought to feeling
  - reflecting on personal development using memories and experiences
- develop language through listening, speaking, reading, writing

My Guide Inside® (Book II) Teacher's Manual

Learning Outcomes

At the end of Chapter 2, learners will show skills and knowledge through:
- an understanding of the principles when
    - listening to their Guide Inside
    - reflecting and reporting on making choices using common sense
    - showing self-determination and natural self-regulation
- participating by listening
- solving a riddle
- communicating creatively and expressively through speaking, writing and art
- discussing and writing about the big picture idea:

You have the gift of thought to use as you choose.
Imagine that!

Resources Tab

myguideinside.com includes Video On Demand Class to bring this chapter to life. Password: mgi

Key Objectives Reminder

Every chapter has two broad learning objectives: Personal Well-being Awareness and Responsibility. With the special focus of Chapter 2, what do the students tell you they have discovered?

Activities

Use Evaluation Rating Scales for art activity, discussion, reflective journal entry, and written output.

Special Resource

Play Dough

My Guide Inside® (Book II) Teacher's Manual

Lesson Plan Chapter 3
Sharing = Caring

Start with Orientation: Find Your Bearings

Tanis' Grandmother says an understanding of the spiritual "gift of thought" shows us choice and that we don't have to act on every thought. At school water spilled on the picture Tanis painted for Grandma's gift; Tanis was angry and worried. Grandma said she was certain Tanis would have another vision and know to paint a lovely picture. Tanis let her mind clear, she felt calm and she envisioned painting new scenes. Tanis felt she and her Grandmother were both giving and receiving. Learners tell when they also let a worry pass. Activities include storytelling, listening and creating gifts of art. Power Words are used in journal entries about the wisdom behind giving and receiving.

This chapter focuses on the choice our Guide Inside offers when we are worried or upset. It shows up as an insight, a thought bringing a better feeling. There is always a chance to feel calm, to naturally self-regulate and be in personal well-being. We can both give and receive; it's a circle of caring and sharing.

Lesson Aims

Chapter 3 aims for learners to:
- increase an understanding of principles by
  – experiencing the relationship of thought choices to well-being
  – discovering value of insights to naturally produce good feelings
- discover value of sharing with a caring adult
- increase awareness of self-determination and natural self-regulation
- invigorate "knowing myself and understanding my world" through discussion
- enhance language development
- develop reading strategies
- experience creativity with writing and art

Learning Opportunities

Chapter 3 is designed to encourage learners to:
- gain an understanding of the principles in terms of
  – letting old thought go and experiencing new thought
  – experiencing insightful thought creating positive feeling
- reflect on the role of thought and choice in sharing and caring relationships
- develop language through listening, speaking, reading, writing

Learning Outcomes

At the end of Chapter 3, learners will show skills and knowledge through:
- an understanding of the principles when
    - reporting on listening to their Guide Inside and choosing to let a thought go
    - sharing awareness of an insight causing a worry to pass
- participating by listening
- communicating creatively and expressively through speaking, writing and art
- discussing and writing about the big picture idea:

Giving and receiving is a circle.

Resources Tab

myguideinside.com includes Video On Demand Class to bring this chapter to life. Password: mgi

Key Objectives Reminder

Every chapter has two broad learning objectives: Personal Well-being Awareness and Responsibility. With the special focus of Chapter 3, what do the students tell you they have discovered?

Activities

Use Evaluation Rating Scales for art activity, discussion, reflective journal entry, and storytelling.

My Guide Inside® (Book II) Teacher's Manual

Lesson Plan Chapter 4
Riding the Wave

Start with Orientation: Find Your Bearings

Koa grew up filled with beautiful feelings until older brother Kimo started demeaning him. Soon Koa lost his joy and everyone saw his bad temper. Before long Koa thought he was not smart, stopped listening to teachers and was angry at nearly everyone. While surfing Koa confided in his uncle who said, "No way!" Koa learned his "light" was covered up with gray "rocks" of negative thoughts. Time to "Huli the bowl!" Students use Power Words, journaling and several activities to reflect on how thought temporarily hides their Guide Inside.

This chapter focuses on the common experience of covering up inner wisdom with too much thinking. As negative thoughts get in the way, feelings go downhill fast. "Huli the bowl" is another way to say, everyone can connect with their Guide Inside.

NOTE: Jane Tucker first heard about the Hawaiian "Bowl of Light" teaching from a local health care professional at a conference on O'ahu in 1996. The "Bowl of Light" metaphor is at the heart of this original story, written in 2002, for students in her Peace Skills class. Years later, she was loaned a copy of *Tales from the Night Rainbow* (cited below) and for the first time, saw the written record of this beautiful traditional teaching.
Tales from the Night Rainbow, Mo'olelo o Na Po Makole: The story of a Woman, a People, and an Island, An oral history as told by Kaili'ohe Kame'ekua of Kamalo, Moloka'i 1816-1931.
Rev. and Engl. Edition, 1990 Pali Jae Lee and Koko Willis, Night Rainbow Publishing Co. Honolulu, HI

Lesson Aims

Chapter 4 aims for learners to:
- gain an understanding of the principles in terms of
  - discovering natural awareness of good feelings
  - learning the changing nature of thoughts
  - experiencing the healthy choice of letting thoughts go as they "*Huli the bowl!*"
  - realizing the impact of thought choices on well-being of self, others, friendships
- gain awareness through sharing with a caring adult
- invigorate "knowing myself and understanding my world" through discussion
- enhance language development
- develop reading strategies
- experience creativity with writing and art

Learning Opportunities
Chapter 4 is designed to encourage learners to:
- gain an understanding of the principles in terms of
    - connecting with their inner wisdom to make wise choices
    - reflecting on powerful knowledge: "Huli the bowl!"
- describe their experiences
- develop language through listening, speaking, reading, writing

Learning Outcomes
At the end of Chapter 4, learners will show skills and knowledge through:
- an understanding of the principles when
    - being aware of a good feeling
    - listening to their Guide Inside
    - trusting a naturally helpful thought leads to well-being
    - experiencing positive feelings like optimism and confidence, and manifesting resilience
- experiencing self-determination and a natural control of impulses regulating behavior
- participating by listening
- communicating creatively and expressively through speaking, writing and art
- discussing and writing about the big picture idea:

Every child is born with a "Bowl of Light" filled with aloha and wisdom.

Resources Tab
myguideinside.com includes Video On Demand Class to bring this chapter to life. Password: mgi

Key Objectives Reminder
Every chapter has two broad learning objectives: Personal Well-being Awareness and Responsibility. With the special focus of Chapter 4, what do the students tell you they have discovered?

Activities
Use Evaluation Rating Scales for art activity, discussion, reflective journal entry, retelling, and written output.

Special Resource
Kaleidoscope

My Guide Inside® (Book II) Teacher's Manual

Lesson Plan Chapter 5
The Best Ship is Friendship

Start with Orientation: Find Your Bearings

Learners encounter two stories. One features Darius and Jerry dealing with a pencil incident in class. Readers are introduced to Darius's insight about a traffic signal visual with red, yellow, green lights reminding him to "Stop!" and let his thinking clear. With that mental "green light" the story replays with a much healthier outcome. Emily and Sofia's story of friendship includes challenges of fearful thinking, worry, even name-calling and a new friend. They discover it is always possible to change your mind and be friends. Discussion and other activities encourage awareness and sharing. Power Words are used in journal entries about making healthy decisions and developing friendships.

This chapter focuses on listening to our Guide Inside. Insights support healthy choices, belonging and friendships. Knowing when to "Stop, Wait, Go" is a quick reminder for using thought in a respectful, kind way.

Lesson Aims

Chapter 5 aims for learners to:
- increase an understanding of principles by
  - listening to inner wisdom to make healthy friendship decisions
  - knowing to remember to "Stop, Wait, Go" with thinking
  - discovering we can change our mind, and have perspective
- show empathy
- explore inclusion
- recognize and accept support
- solve problems peacefully
- invigorate "knowing myself and understanding my world" through discussion
- enhance language development
- develop reading strategies
- experience creativity with personal writing and art

Learning Opportunities

Chapter 5 is designed to encourage learners to:
- gain an understanding of the principles in terms of
  - identifying opportunities to make healthy decisions
  - identifying positive ways to make and keep healthy friendships
- develop language through listening, speaking, reading, writing

Learner Outcomes

At the end of Chapter 5, learners will show skills and knowledge through:
- an understanding of the principles when
    - using their Guide Inside in making choices
    - acting from calm thinking with empathy and kindness
    - stopping before acting on impulsive thoughts
    - having perspective and realizing they can change their mind
- participating by listening
- communicating creatively and expressively through speaking, writing and art
- experiencing self-determination and a natural control of impulses regulating behavior
- beginning and keeping healthy friendships
- making respectful decisions based on well-being of self and others
- solving problems peacefully
- discussing and writing about the big picture idea:

We can make healthy decisions and
make and keep healthy friendships.

Resources Tab

myguideinside.com includes Video On Demand Class to bring this chapter to life. Password: mgi

Key Objectives Reminder

Every chapter has two broad learning objectives: Personal Well-being Awareness and Responsibility. With the special focus of Chapter 5, what do the students tell you they have discovered?

Activities

Use *Evaluation Rating Scales* for discussion, poster activity, reflective journal entry, and sharing activity.

My Guide Inside® (Book II) Teacher's Manual

Lesson Plan Chapter 6
What a Difference an Insight Makes

Start with Orientation: Find Your Bearings

Jake quickly got the hang of skateboarding. Even older kids watched and were amazed. Jake got to thinking kids really liked him because of it. A new boy named Carlos could match him and do many new things. Kids started watching Carlos; Jake got shaky, sick and stayed away. Jake's Grandpa said Carlos's performance didn't take anything away from Jake. He realized it is what's inside that counts; being helpful, welcoming and fun. Discussion and activities stress mastering a new skill is easy and fun. Power Words are used to write about who and what they are inside.

This chapter focuses on finding personal well-being inside, knowing who and what we are. Negative thought results in us forgetting what's inside. Insights lead to good choices and a new way of seeing things which invigorates well-being and learning.

Lesson Aims

Chapter 6 aims for learners to:
- increase an understanding of principles by
    - trusting who and what they are inside
    - using inner wisdom
    - experiencing the value of insight, having perspective
- be inclusive
- recognize and accept family support
- invigorate "knowing myself and understanding my world" through discussion
- enhance language development
- develop reading strategies
- experience creativity with personal writing and art

Learning Opportunities

Chapter 6 is designed to encourage learners to:
- gain an understanding of the principles in terms of
    - continuing to identify opportunities to make healthy decisions
    - making respectful thought choices based on well-being of self and others
- develop language through listening, speaking, reading, writing

My Guide Inside® (Book II) Teacher's Manual

Learner Outcomes
At the end of Chapter 6, learners will show skills and knowledge through:
- an understanding of the principles when
    - making healthy choices
    - using insights and having new perspectives
- enjoying who they are
- participating by listening
- treating others respectfully
- recognizing and accepting support
- communicating creatively and expressively through speaking, writing and art
- beginning and keeping healthy friendships
- discussing and writing about the big picture idea:

Who and what you are inside is what counts.

Resources Tab
myguideinside.com includes Video On Demand Class to bring this chapter to life. Password: mgi

Key Objectives Reminder
Every chapter has two broad learning objectives: Personal Well-being Awareness and Responsibility. With the special focus of Chapter 6, what do the students tell you they have discovered?

Activities
Use *Evaluation Rating Scales* for art, discussion, and reflective journal entry.

Special Resource
String
Video instructions for Cat's Cradle: http://youtube.com/watch?v=VpHTPnrYLzQ

Lesson Plan Chapter 7
Wheels of Learning Keep on Turning

Start with Orientation: Find Your Bearings

Amara loved life. She was playful, imaginative and always learning something. A cousin told her to be more serious, to "buckle down." Another worried about running out of time. Her brother said to put herself first. Amara began thinking like this and soon was very unhappy. She noticed her baby brother giggle as a rubber ducky kept popping up in the kiddie pool. Amara's mind cleared a bit. Then her insight came, "My happiness keeps popping up!" Her Guide Inside helped her decide to keep that thought alive. Amara experienced resilience and the wheel of learning was turning effortlessly again. She naturally showed confidence and optimism. Power Words are used when reflecting on thoughts affecting happiness.

This chapter focuses on recognizing a good feeling or state of mind. Learners discover the important role our Guide Inside plays in signaling any shift to an unhappy state. An insight brings a new motivating idea and a shift to happiness, playfulness, enjoyment and learning is easier.

Lesson Aims

Chapter 7 aims for learners to:
- increase an understanding of principles by
  - discovering joy can be experienced
  - realizing we sometimes innocently "follow the leader" into negative thoughts
  - relying on insights from my **Guide Inside** to lead to happiness
- enhance self-determination and self-regulation
- experience confidence and optimism
- recognize and accept family support
- make respectful thought choices based on well-being of self
- invigorate "knowing myself and understanding my world" through discussion
- enhance language development
- develop reading strategies
- experience creativity with personal writing and art

Learning Opportunities
Chapter 7 is designed to encourage learners to:
- gain an understanding of the principles in terms of
  - gaining awareness of natural resilience, following new insights
- reflect on the power of thought to create ideas as well as their experience
- develop language through listening, speaking, reading, writing

Learner Outcomes
At the end of Chapter 7, learners will show skills and knowledge through:
- an understanding of the principles when
  - being aware of changes in their feelings
  - instinctively listening to their Guide Inside
  - acting on helpful insights and experience an improved feeling, state of mind
  - experiencing natural motivation
- participating by listening
- gaining in self-efficacy, awareness of abilities, strengths
- communicating creatively and expressively through speaking, writing and art
- competently discussing and writing about the big picture idea:

"Sometimes it was only their thoughts that were making them unhappy and if they could understand…, it would help make them feel well."

(Banks, 2004, p. 46)

Resources Tab
myguideinside.com includes Video On Demand Class to bring this chapter to life. Password: mgi

Key Objectives Reminder
Every chapter has two broad learning objectives: Personal Well-being Awareness and Responsibility. With the special focus of Chapter 7, what do the students tell you they have discovered?

Activities
Use *Evaluation Rating Scales* for art activity, discussion, poem writing, poem reciting, and reflective journal entry.

Special Resource
Balloons

Lesson Plan Chapter 8
You are a Wonder

Start with Orientation: Find Your Bearings

In last session learners use their own words to describe the personal impact of their MGI journey. Various activities review key themes such as:
- ➢ *My Guide Inside* is always present.
- ➢ *As soon as the cloudy thought passes, there is a new, nicer thought.*
- ➢ *Discovering my Guide Inside is knowledge, which grows with us, brings love and compassion and leads to happiness.*
- ➢ *We can drop a thought like a hot potato.*
- ➢ *Every child is born with a "Bowl of Light" filled with aloha and wisdom.*
- ➢ *Thought is a gift and we have the choice of which thoughts to act on.*
- ➢ *In a state of well-being, we are welcoming, friendly and kind; it is easy to learn and also to make and keep friendships.*
- ➢ *Insights help us know ourselves and understand our world.*
- ➢ *Learners gain confidence and optimism, awareness of their abilities and strengths.*
- ➢ *Learners understand how they operate from the inside out.*
- ➢ *They recognize and accept family, school, and community support.*

This final lesson focuses on review and reflection. Learners describe their development in this course. Ultimately listening to my Guide Inside, understanding the power of thought, and trusting insights becomes a way of life. Personal awareness and responsibility are natural outcomes.

Learner Post-Assessment, found in this manual or at myguideinside.com, is to be completed at the end of this last lesson. See details below.

Lesson Aims

Chapter 8 aims for learners to:
- increase understanding of principles by
  - reflecting on principles lessons learned
  - seeing the "big picture" of change in themselves
- gain awareness of capabilities, strengths (self-efficacy)
- communicate an understanding of making healthy decisions for long term
- recognize family, school and community support

My Guide Inside® (Book II) Teacher's Manual

- continue to use reading strategies
- invigorate "knowing myself and understanding my world" through discussion
- continue to develop language through listening, speaking, reading, and writing
- realize personal ability in writing and art

Learning Opportunities

Chapter 8 is designed to encourage learners to:
- gain an understanding of the principles in terms of
  - having perspective
  - reflecting what they have learned in *My Guide Inside*
  - reflecting on their capabilities, strengths, well-being and their circle of support
- develop language through listening, speaking, reading, writing

Learning Outcomes

At the end of Chapter 8, learners will show skills and knowledge through an understanding of the *principles and related competencies* when they:
- communicate, in varied ways, how they know themselves and understand their world
  - communicate creatively and expressively through speaking and writing
  - demonstrate self-efficacy with confidence and optimism in their ability to learn, make and keep friends
  - demonstrate personal awareness, well-being and responsibility they attribute to knowing their Guide Inside, understanding thought and using insights
  - show respect for self, family and community
  - naturally self-regulate by listening to their common sense before acting
- competently discussing and writing about the big picture idea:

> *"It is never too late to dream, and if your heart and thoughts are pure your dreams can come true."*
>
> (Banks, 2004, p. 68)

Resources Tab

myguideinside.com includes Video On Demand Class to bring this chapter to life. Password: mgi

Key Objectives Reminder

Every chapter has two broad learning objectives: Personal Well-being Awareness and Responsibility. With the special focus of Chapter 8, what do the students tell you they have discovered?

Activities

Use *Evaluation Rating Scales* provided for mind map, personal metaphor, and reflective journal entry.

Learner Post-Assessment Details

After students complete *MGI II Post Assessments*, they may compare to their original *MGI Pre-Assessments* to see and discuss progress with teacher or full group. This self-evaluation captures results in the two broad *MGI* objectives: **(1)** Personal Well-being Awareness and **(2)** Communication, Thinking, Personal and Social Responsibility. Additional information follows.

My Guide Inside® (Book II) Teacher's Manual

Lesson Plan Chapter 9
Power Words

Start with Orientation: Find Your Bearings
This last chapter lists important vocabulary building Power Words used in each of the preceding chapters. Refer learners to these pages to find the meaning of these key words and develop their expressive language. Chapter word lists may also be used as thought starters for small discussion groups and written reflections.

Excellent Supplement to *My Guide Inside*
After completing **MGI**, you might want to follow up with this special book.
The novel, *Dear Liza*, by Sydney Banks (2004) is an excellent children's story to enjoy before, during, or after completing **My Guide Inside**. From the back cover of the book *Dear Liza*:

"In this charming, heartwarming novel, Sydney Banks weaves an unforgettable tale of a poor yet happy orphan girl living in the slums of 19th-century London. From treasured letters left to her by her mother, Liza learns a unique understanding about life. In her special way, her quiet wisdom touches the hearts and lives of everyone she meets."

Your Own Favorites
In addition, as a classroom teacher, you may find your own favorite books to continue teaching about the principles introduced in **My Guide Inside**. The principles are elemental and therefore connect to any story or book.

Final Note to Teachers
When you have completed this class do take time to reflect on what you have done well and what you might try in the future. Especially pay attention to what your own wisdom reveals about your teaching experience with **My Guide Inside**. How has it impacted not only your students, but you yourself? Sydney Banks advises us to exercise our choice and find inner wisdom for ourselves. Once found, we naturally share and we are advised by John Hattie to know our impact. Now that's simple logic. Congratulations on making a difference in the world!

Assessment and Evaluation Rating Scales

First Class:

- Learners complete the *MGI II Pre- and Post-Assessment* prior to the first lesson. Please do a few samples to ensure students understand how to complete the assessment. Provide reading support as needed.

All Classes:

- Teacher uses appropriate criteria from *Evaluation Rating Scales for Activities*.

Final Class:

- Learners repeat the *MGI II Pre- and Post-Assessment*.

    Teacher completes **"Snapshot" Learner Observations**.

    Teacher and students compare **Learner Pre- and Post-Assessment** results and discuss highlights of these outcomes. This may be done individually or as a group. Especially note increased personal awareness, understanding, well-being and responsibility. Conclude with a celebration and commitment to use my *Guide Inside* throughout life. (Teachers included!)

    Special Note: When possible, a school district research office staffer may develop an efficient computerized system for Pre- and Post-Assessment data collection, analysis and reporting to the classroom teacher. Both individual student and full class digital reports may be developed. It may be helpful to share results with appropriate school building or district officials for purposes of program evaluation and planning.

Learner *MGI II* Pre- and Post Assessment

Class_____ ID_____ Date_____

Please complete a copy of this survey before the first chapter *and* a copy after the last chapter!

Circle the answer that is true for you for each statement	Almost Never	A Little	Some	Mostly	A Lot
1. I am happy with my life.	Almost Never	A Little	Some	Mostly	A Lot
2. I wait for good ideas to pop into my head.	Almost Never	A Little	Some	Mostly	A Lot
3. When I worry I let it go.	Almost Never	A Little	Some	Mostly	A Lot
4. I make friends easily.	Almost Never	A Little	Some	Mostly	A Lot
5. I think too much.	Almost Never	A Little	Some	Mostly	A Lot
6. I like who I am.	Almost Never	A Little	Some	Mostly	A Lot
7. I catch myself when I am getting upset.	Almost Never	A Little	Some	Mostly	A Lot
8. I am a good student.	Almost Never	A Little	Some	Mostly	A Lot
9. I know who to ask for help.	Almost Never	A Little	Some	Mostly	A Lot
10. I stay out of conflicts with others.	Almost Never	A Little	Some	Mostly	A Lot
11. I like my feelings.	Almost Never	A Little	Some	Mostly	A Lot
12. Deep inside I know the right thing to do.	Almost Never	A Little	Some	Mostly	A Lot

After you complete this entire class, please also answer this one question. Thank you!

What is the most important thing you learned from *MGI* that has really helped you out?"

My Guide Inside® (Book II) Teacher's Manual

Teacher "Snapshot" Learner Observations

Prior to completing this form, review each student's progress based on a comparison of their Pre- to Post- Assessments. Reflect and then complete this "Snapshot" to record your main observations. Take time with each student to hear his or her sense of personal progress. Then share your observations.

Name: _____   Date: _____

PERSONAL WELL-BEING AWARENESS

Almost Never   **1**   **2**   **3**   **4**   **5**   A Lot

Observations

COMMUNICATION, THINKING, PERSONAL AND SOCIAL RESPONSIBILITY

Almost Never   **1**   **2**   **3**   **4**   **5**   A Lot

Observations

RELEVANT STUDENT INFORMATION

School Attendance
Not yet within Expectations   **1**   **2**   **3**   **4**   **5**   Fully Meets Expectations

Classroom academic performance
Not yet within Expectations   **1**   **2**   **3**   **4**   **5**   Fully Meets Expectations

Social behavior in and out of classroom
Not yet within Expectations   **1**   **2**   **3**   **4**   **5**   Fully Meets Expectations

Participation in class
Not yet within Expectations   **1**   **2**   **3**   **4**   **5**   Fully Meets Expectations

Observations:

My Guide Inside® (Book II) Teacher's Manual

Evaluation Rating Scales for Activities

Name: _____ Chapter: _____

Evaluation Scale:

5	Exceptionally good; clearly meets or exceeds all criteria
4	Very Good; meets all criteria and exceeds some criteria
3	Good; meets all criteria
2	Less than Acceptable; meets some criteria; provide support
1	Limited; meets few criteria, in progress; provide adaptations/modifications

Art Criteria	5	4	3	2	1
<ul><li>original</li><li>captures essence</li><li>effective use of space</li><li>colorful, shaded or use of ink</li></ul>					
Belonging Map Criteria	5	4	3	2	1
<ul><li>thoughtful</li><li>shows connections</li><li>accurate</li><li>legible</li></ul>					
Discussion Criteria	5	4	3	2	1
<ul><li>unbiased toward other people</li><li>respectful toward others' viewpoints</li><li>shares own viewpoint</li><li>can see "bigger picture"</li></ul>					
Mural Criteria	5	4	3	2	1
<ul><li>clear, neat</li><li>effective use of space</li><li>colorful</li><li>accurate</li></ul>					
Personal Metaphor Criteria	5	4	3	2	1
<ul><li>image has impact</li><li>authentic qualities</li><li>effective use of space</li><li>neat</li></ul>					
Poem Writing Criteria	5	4	3	2	1
<ul><li>shows depth of thought</li><li>organized</li><li>descriptive language</li><li>creates a mood</li></ul>					

Evaluation Rating Scales for Activities (continued)

Poem Reciting Criteria	5	4	3	2	1
<ul><li>prepared</li><li>accurate</li><li>speaks clearly</li><li>confident</li></ul>					
Poster Criteria	5	4	3	2	1
<ul><li>informative, neat</li><li>effective use of space</li><li>colorful</li><li>accurate</li></ul>					
Reflection Journal Criteria	5	4	3	2	1
<ul><li>uses "I"</li><li>thoughtful</li><li>shows connections</li><li>shows insight</li></ul>					
Retelling Criteria	5	4	3	2	1
<ul><li>demonstrates willingness</li><li>participates actively</li><li>states logical beginning, middle, and end</li><li>possesses confidence</li></ul>					
Sharing Criteria	5	4	3	2	1
<ul><li>demonstrates willingness</li><li>expresses ideas clearly</li><li>possesses confidence</li><li>communicates effectively</li></ul>					
Written Output Criteria	5	4	3	2	1
<ul><li>depth of thought</li><li>detail</li><li>logical</li><li>communicates effectively</li><li>correct conventions</li></ul>					

My Guide Inside® (Book II) Teacher's Manual

Integrating My Guide Inside in Education

Undoubtedly, as an educator you are responsible for meeting official learning objectives and student competency standards. ***My Guide Inside*** is designed to help you do that. ***My Guide Inside*** meets educational learning objectives and competency requirements.

Current Education Policy Context
As we write this *Teacher's Manual*, the British Columbia Ministry of Education in Canada is developing a new curriculum including, "Personal Awareness and Responsibility Competence Profile." **MGI** aligns with these innovative guidelines.

The most current version of that work states, "Personal awareness and responsibility is one of the three interrelated competencies that relate to the broad area of Social and Emotional Learning." The curriculum further explains Personal Awareness and Responsibility competency involves: Self-determination, Self-regulation, and Well-being. The Ministry discusses Well-being this way:

> *"Students who are personally aware and responsible recognize how their decisions and actions affect their mental, physical, emotional, social, cognitive, and spiritual wellness, and take increasing responsibility for caring for themselves. They keep themselves healthy and physically active, manage stress, and express a sense of personal well-being. ... They recognize the importance of happiness, and have strategies that help them find peace in challenging situations."*

(Personal Awareness and Responsibility Competence Profiles, p. 3)

There is also an interest in promoting well-being in the United Kingdom's schools. According to "Promoting Fundamental British Values as part of SMSC in Schools," schools must "promote the spiritual, moral, social and cultural (SMSC) development of their pupils." At this time there is increasing awareness globally of the need for all education systems to support and foster lifelong well-being of students. In that sense this comprehensive Pre-K-12 ***My Guide Inside*** curriculum is a timely resource for all educators and their school systems.

Regardless of where you are located in the world, this material is suited for and meets selected requirements for English Language Arts (ELA), Health Education, Career Education, and Personal, Social, Health and Economic Education (PSHE). It supports inclusion and may be used to develop competencies in Communication (C), Thinking (T) and Social Emotional Learning (SEL), which includes decision making, self-management, healthy relationships and well-being. It also may be used to develop competencies in Personal and Social Responsibility (PS), which includes positive personal and cultural identity, personal awareness and responsibility, spiritual wellness, as well as social responsibility.

Learners everywhere can discover my *Guide Inside*, also referred to simply as common sense or wisdom. They become increasingly aware of and take responsibility for thoughts and actions that impact their intellectual, creative, social, emotional and physical potentials as well as their spiritual wellness. Accessing natural inner wisdom produces joy, love, compassion, personal strength, and leads to academic success. The principles on which this curriculum is based are the key to innate mental health characterized by optimism, resilience, and well-being.

Understanding these principles actually supports and increases a student's well-being, self-efficacy and self-confidence; and improves ability to self-regulate, set goals, and take responsibilities for their choices and actions. With understanding, students become patient learning over time, persevere in difficult situations to solve problems calmly, and realize the logic of how their actions affect themselves and others.

Objectives of My Guide Inside

The principles operate in all people, including every student. This MGI curriculum points the way to wholeness, happiness, creativity and well-being in all parts of life.
Therefore, *MGI* has these two academic goals:
(1) to enhance Personal Well-being, key to learning, with an understanding of these principles, and
(2) to develop competencies in Communication, Thinking, as well as Personal and Social Awareness and Responsibility (SEL).
MGI accomplishes both goals by using stories, discussion and various written and creative activities, as it increases competency in English Language Arts, including Digital Media.

Discovering our *Guide Inside* enhances ability to make decisions, navigate life and build healthy relationships. *MGI* accomplishes its objectives by using age appropriate stories, discussion and various written and creative activities, as it increases competency in English Language Arts.

My Guide Inside® (Book II) Teacher's Manual

Educational Learning Objectives and Competencies

My Guide Inside curriculum also meets these additional requirements common to most school systems globally as detailed below.

English Language Arts Objectives
Reading and Viewing: Learners will expand their knowledge and apply strategies to understand, compare ideas with prior knowledge, make inferences, reflect, and respond. Learners will enhance their vocabulary while they read and view for enjoyment, to explore ideas and to inspire creativity. They will synthesize texts to create insight and communicate viewpoints to expand thinking.

Writing and Representation: Learners will expand their communication and create meaningful texts, including visual texts, that show depth of thought and have a logical sequence. Learners will refine texts with enhanced vocabulary, clear language and correct conventions of grammar, spelling and punctuation. Learners will use an engaging "voice" and present texts in a variety of ways.

Oral Language: Listening and speaking are foundations of language learning for developing vocabulary, making connections and having perspective. Learners will expand knowledge by listening to others as well as realizing what they themselves know by reflecting, expressing their own point of view and communicating through oral language. Learners will rehearse and perform to produce language and discuss language meaning.

Career Education and Health Education Objectives
Learners will practice respectful, ethical, inclusive behavior which is preparation for the workplace. Learners will respond suitably to discrimination and harassment, show respect and understand what makes and maintains a healthy relationship. Learners will identify supportive relationships, healthy thoughts and feelings, and understand personal safety. Learners will access knowledge to support healthy decisions.

Communication Competency
Learners will share with others in conversation to develop understanding and relationships. Learners will communicate and collaborate on activities, including effective use of Digital Media, to present their work. Students will acquire knowledge and share what they have learned through presentations, self-monitoring and self-assessment.

Personal and Social Competencies (Social and Emotional Learning)
Personal Awareness and Responsibility: Learners can anticipate results of own actions. They understand and become increasingly aware of and take responsibility for thoughts and actions that impact their intellectual, creative, social, emotional and physical

potentials, as well as their spiritual wellness. They are flexible; making responsible decisions about which thoughts to act on, based on well-being of self and others.

- **Well-being**: Through an understanding of my guide inside, ever-present natural inner wisdom or common sense, learners take increasing responsibility for their personal well-being, which includes their safety and happiness. Learners understand that mental health is a state of well-being.
- **Self-Determination**: Learners understand the cause and effect rule that thought creates feeling and thought is the "seed" of behavior. Learners have confidence, an awareness of strengths to face challenges and know to access compassion. Learners advocate for themselves.
- **Self-Regulation**: Learners choose their guide inside (their own natural inner wisdom) to regulate behavior effectively and control impulses. Learners show honesty, motivate themselves and work toward achieving success.

Social Awareness and Responsibility: Learners are fair, appreciate others' perspectives and solve problems in peaceful ways. They show empathy, compassion and understanding, and are inclusive and contribute to the community.

- **Healthy Relationships**: Learners listen, co-operate and communicate clearly. They show compassion, empathy and understanding, solve people problems calmly, and seek and offer help when needed.

Positive Personal and Cultural Identity: Learners understand their identity evolves as they gain understanding and experience in life. Learners see that natural inner wisdom combined with personal attributes can help them navigate life. Learners identify people who can support them as well as see that they can also offer help.

Thinking Competency
Learners will gain awareness of the power of thought, which is the thinking process in action. Via creative thinking, they will generate ideas while investigating relevance and connection to "Big Picture" ideas. They will learn that their ideas have value. Learners will understand to let the personal mind clear to allow new thought to emerge. They will have opportunities to develop new ideas, insights, that change what they do in life. Via reflective and critical thinking, learners will choose which thoughts to pay attention to, which logically lead to intended outcomes.

Supplemental Resources

Recommended Three Principles Resources

By Sydney Banks:
Books
Second Chance (1983)
In Quest of the Pearl (1989)
The Missing Link: Reflections on Philosophy and Spirit (1998)
The Enlightened Gardener (2001)
Dear Liza (2004)
The Enlightened Gardener Revisited (2005).
CDs

Attitude!	*In Quest of the Pearl*	*Second Chance*
Great Spirit, The	*Long Beach Lectures*	*Washington Lectures*
Hawaii Lectures	*One Thought Away*	*What is Truth*

DVDs
Hawaii Lectures (1-4)
Long Beach Lectures (1-4)
Washington Lectures (1-2)
The Ultimate Answer

See www.sydbanks.com and Sydney Banks Videos:https://www.youtube.com/@sydney-banks3/videos

Continued Learning for Educators

The Power of the Three Principles in Schools Four-part free online professional development series for educators created by Christa Campsall and Barb Aust. This series links to Sydney Banks Long Beach Lectures.
www.myguideinside.com

Long Beach Lectures (1-4) video series of presentations by Sydney Banks
www.sydbanks.com/longbeach/

Marshall, K. (2021). *Discovering Resilience and Well-being in School Communities.* In: Nabors, L. (eds) Resilient Children. Springer Series on Child and Family Studies. Springer, Cham. https://doi.org/10.1007/978-3-030-81728-2_5

Educators Living in the Joy of Gratitude (Free recorded professional development programs facilitated by Kathy Marshall Emerson.)
www.nationalresilienceresource.com/Educator-Preparation.html

Current links to webinars with Christa Campsall
www.myguideinside.com

Selected Principles Publications for Educators

Aust, B. (2016). Field notes: Capturing the moment with a story. *ASCD Express.* Retrieved from www.ascd.org/ascd-express/vol12/1207-aust.aspx

Aust, B. (2013). *The essential curriculum: 21 ideas for developing a positive and optimistic culture.* Author.

Aust, B., & Vine, W. (2003, October). The power of voice in schools. ASCD *Classroom Leadership,* 7, 5, 8.

Campsall, C. (2005). Increasing student sense of feeling safe: The role of thought and common sense in developing social responsibility. Unpublished master's thesis. Royal Roads University, Victoria, British Columbia, Canada.

Marshall Emerson, K. (2015). "Resilience research and community practice: A view from the bridge." Paper presented to the Pathways to Resilience III, 6/19/2015, Halifax, Nova Scotia.

Marshall, K. (2005, September). Resilience in our schools: Discovering mental health and hope from the inside-out. In D. L. White, M. K. Faber, & B. C. Glenn (Eds.). *Proceedings of Persistently Safe Schools 2005.* 128-140. Washington, DC: Hamilton Fish Institute, The George Washington University for U. S. Department of Justice, Office of Juvenile Justice and Delinquency Prevention.

Marshall, K. (2004). Resilience research and practice: National Resilience Resource Center bridging the gap. In H. C. Waxman, Y. N. Padron and J. Gray (Eds.). *Educational resiliency: student, teacher, and school perspectives.* Pp. 63-84. Greenwich, CT: Information Age Publishing.

Marshall, K. (November, 1998). Reculturing systems with resilience/health realization. *Promoting positive and healthy behaviors in children: Fourteenth annual Rosalynn Carter symposium on mental health Policy.* Atlanta, GA: The Carter Center, pp. 48-58.

Websites

3 Principles Ed Talks: www.myguideinside.com
National Resilience Resource Center: www.nationalresilienceresource.com
Sydney Banks: www.sydneybanks.org

MGI in Context of Current Research and Theory

The *MGI* comprehensive Pre-K-12 curriculum was developed to complement evidence based approaches to effective education and foster student resilience. *MGI* theory stands on the shoulders of significant educational and other relevant researchers such as, but not limited to: Bonnie Benard, Faye Brownlie, Robert Coles, Richard Davidson, Cheryl Dweck, Jenni Donohoo, Michael Fullan, John Hattie, Ann Masten, Parker Palmer, Michael Rutter, Leyton Schnellert, George Villiant, Roger Weissberg, Emmy Werner, Steven and Sybil Wolin.

In every country there are experts dedicated to bringing out the best in students. For example, with leadership of Kathy Marshall Emerson, the National Resilience Resource Center sees every youth as at promise rather than as at risk.

MGI focuses on simple principles operating in all students. Its objectives point to the promise inside every student to: **(1)** enhance Personal Well-being, and **(2)** develop Communication, Thinking, Social Emotional Learning, and Personal and Social Responsibility competencies. These general objectives may be customized to fit specific countries, systems, schools or classrooms.

Authors Barbara Aust and Kathy Marshall Emerson, education and resilience veterans, guided *MGI* conceptual development to clarify the "fit" between *MGI* and established cutting edge global educational efforts and research. These sample resources laying out the "Big Picture" in *MGI* may be especially helpful in discovering this alignment:

- "Personal Awareness and Responsibility Competency Profiles" from British Columbia's Ministry of Education provides the basis for *MGI* learning objectives at https://curriculum.gov.bc.ca
- "Fitting in with Other Programs" at http://www.nationalresilienceresource.com/Fitting-In.html suggests how principles curriculum like *MGI* complements existing school initiatives and programs.
- "Educators Living in the Joy of Gratitude," facilitated by Kathy Marshall Emerson, includes 12 presentations by veteran educators describing learning, living and sharing the principles in schools globally for the last 40 years. Available from: www.nationalre-silienceresource.com/Educator-Preparation.html
- *MGI* rests on an essential research base such as "References Relevant to BC's

Curriculum Assessment and Transformation" at https://curriculum.gov.bc.ca

For a deeper examination of relevant research see selections below.

ADDITIONAL SCHOLARLY PUBLICATIONS

Education Research and Theory

Berk, L. (2007). *Development through the lifespan.* Boston: Allyn and Bacon.

Brownlie, F., & Schnellert, L. (2009). *It's all about thinking: Collaborating to support all learners.* Winnipeg, MB: Portage & Main Press.

Cicchetti, D., Rappaport, I., Weissberg, R. (Eds.). (2006). *The promotion of wellness in children and adolescents.* Child Welfare League of America. Washington, D.C.: CWLA Press.

Coles, R. (1990). *The spiritual life of children.* Boston: Houghton Mifflin Company.

Donohoo, J. (2016). Collective efficacy: *How educators' beliefs impact student learning.* Thousand Oaks: Corwin Press.

Dweck, C. (2006). *Mindset: The new psychology of success.* New York, NY: Random House.

Fullan, M. (2016). *Indelible leadership: Always leave them learning.* Thousand Oaks, CA: Corwin Press.

Fullan, M. (2001). *Leading in a culture of change.* San Francisco, Jossey-Bass.

Hattie, J. (2015). The applicability of visible learning to higher education. Scholarship of teaching and learning in psychology, 1(1), 79-91.

Hattie, J. (2011). *Visible learning for teachers: Maximizing impact on learning.* New York, NY: Routledge.

Hattie, J. (2009). *Visible learning: A synthesis of over 800 meta-analyses relating to achievement.* New York, NY: Routledge.

Palmer, P. (1998). *The courage to teach: Exploring the inner landscape of a teacher's life.* San Francisco: Jossey-Bass Publishing.

Reclaiming Youth International. (1990). *Circle of courage.* Retrieved from https://www.starr.org/training/youth/aboutcircleofcourage

Roehlkepartain, E., King, P., Wagener, L., & Benson, P. (Eds.). (2006). *The handbook of spiritual development in childhood and adolescence.* Thousand Oaks, CA: Sage Publications.

Schnellert, L., Widdess, N., & Watson, L. (2015). *It's all about thinking: Creating pathways for all learners in middle years.* Winnipeg, MB: Portage & Main Press.

Resilience Research and Theory

Benard, B. (2004). *Resiliency: What we have learned.* Oakland, CA: West Ed.

Benard, B. (1991). *Fostering resiliency in kids: Protective factors in the family, school, and community.* Portland, OR: Northwest Regional Educational Laboratory.

Benard, B. & Marshall, K. (1997). A framework for practice: Tapping innate resilience. *Research/Practice*, Minneapolis: University of Minnesota, Center for Applied Research and Educational Improvement, Spring, pp. 9-15.

Davidson, R. J., & Begley, S. (2012). *The emotional life of your brain: How its unique patterns affect the way you think, feel and live – How you can change them.* New York: Hudson Street Press.

Marshall, K. (2004). Resilience research and practice: National Resilience Resource Center bridging the gap. In H. C. Waxman, Y. N. Padron and J. Gray (Eds.). *Educational resiliency: student, teacher, and school perspectives*. Pp. 63-84. Greenwich, CT: Information Age Publishing.

Marshall, K. (November, 1998). Reculturing systems with resilience/health realization. *Promoting positive and healthy behaviors in children: Fourteenth annual Rosalynn Carter symposium on mental health policy*. Atlanta, GA: The Carter Center, pp. 48-58.

Masten, A. (2014). *Ordinary magic: Resilience processes in development.* New York, NY: Guilford Press.

Rutter, M. (1990). Psychosocial resilience and protective mechanisms. In D. Ciccetti, A. Masten, K. Neuchterlein, J. Rolf, & S. Weintraub (Eds.), *Risk and protective factors in the development of psychopathology* (pp.181-214). New York: Cambridge University Press.

Shapiro, S. & Carlson, L. (2009). *The art and science of mindfulness: Integrating mindfulness into psychology and the helping professions.* Washington, DC: American Psychological Association.

Sternberg, E., (2001). *The balance within: The science connecting health and emotions.* New York, NY: W.H. Freeman & Co.

Vaillant, G. (2012).*Triumphs of experience: The men of the Harvard grant study.* Cambridge: The Belknap Press of Harvard University Press.

Werner, E. & Smith, R., (2001).Journeys from childhood to midlife: Overcoming the odds. Ithaca, NY: Cornell University Press.

Werner, E. (2005). What can we learn about resilience from large-scale longitudinal studies? In S. Goldstein & R. Brooks (Eds.), *Handbook of resilience in children* (91-106). New York, NY: Kluwer Academic/Plenum.

Wolin, S.J. & Wolin, S. (1993). *The resilient self: How survivors of troubled families rise above adversity.* New York, NY: Villard Books

Three Principles in Education

Aust, B. (2016). Field notes: Capturing the moment with a story. *ASCD Express*. Retrieved from www.ascd.org/ascd-express/vol12/1207-aust.aspx

Aust, B. (2013). *The essential curriculum: 21 ideas for developing a positive and optimistic culture.* Author.

Aust, B., & Vine, W. (2003, October). The power of voice in schools. *ASCD Classroom Leadership*, 7, 5, 8.

Campsall, C. (2005). Increasing student sense of feeling safe: The role of thought and common sense in developing social responsibility. Unpublished master's thesis. Royal Roads University, Victoria, British Columbia, Canada.

Marshall Emerson, K. (2015). "Resilience research and community practice: A view from the bridge." Paper presented to the Pathways to Resilience III, 6/19/2015, Halifax, Nova Scotia.

Marshall K. (2021) Discovering Resilience and Well-being in School Communities. In: Nabors L. (eds) Resilient Children. Springer Series on Child and Family Studies. Springer, Cham. https://rdcu.be/cMsYf

Marshall, K. (2005, September). Resilience in our schools: Discovering mental health and hope from the inside-out. In D. L. White, M. K. Faber, & B. C. Glenn (Eds.). *Proceedings of Persistently Safe Schools 2005.* 128-140. Washington, DC: Hamilton Fish Institute, The George Washington University for U. S. Department of Justice, Office of Juvenile Justice and Delinquency Prevention.

Roots of *MGI*

MGI is the first principles-based comprehensive school curriculum. The earliest educators to quietly carry the principles into their schools—Barbara Aust and Christa Campsall—began learning from Sydney Banks in 1975 in British Columbia. Jane Tucker and Bob Campsall also began to learn from Sydney Banks in the mid-1970's and all have worked in schools directly with students for many years. By 1993 Kathy Marshall Emerson of the National Resilience Resource Center was integrating the principles in two 20-year school community projects in America. By 2016 the Educators Living in the Joy of Gratitude global webinar series documented the experiences of veteran Pre-K-12 educators sharing the principles "inside the schoolhouse."

The outcomes of learning, living and then sharing the principles in education complement many efforts to effectively transform education at all levels. There is growing interest in integrating the principles in education globally. To be successful these efforts must be in alignment with applicable, current curriculum standards in any location; in some cases widely accepted research-based papers provide the bests guidance. Most countries have easily accessible guidelines. These are samples:

American Common Core State Standards Initiative. (2017). *About the Standards.* Retrieved from www.corestandards.org.
BC Ministry of Education. (2024). *BC's Curriculum.* Retrieved from www.curriculum.gov.bc.ca
BC Ministry of Education. (2024). *Personal Awareness and Responsibility Competency Profiles.* Retrieved from www.curriculum.gov.bc.ca
"Collaborative for Academic, Social, and Emotional Learning (CASEL). (2017)." *Core SEL Competencies.* Retrieved from http://www.casel.org/core-competencies/
National Education Policy, 2020 India. *Aiming at Holistic Development of Learners* https://www.education.gov.in/sites/upload_files/mhrd/files/NEP_Final_English_0.pdf
"Personal, Social, Health and Economic (PSHE) Education." *Gov.UK.* Retrieved from http://www.gov.uk
"Promoting Fundamental British Values as part of SMSC in Schools" (2014). *Gov.UK.* Retrieved from http://www.gov.uk
"Secondary National Curriculum." 02 Dec. (2014). Gov.UK. Retrieved from http://www.gov.uk

Acknowledgments

Sydney Banks deeply cared about young people. He knew that if we could help our youth, the world would be "a far, far better place." He was an ordinary man who had an experience that profoundly changed him from the inside-out. For the rest of his life, as a speaker and author, he was dedicated to sharing the universal Three Principles he uncovered: Mind, Consciousness and Thought.

As teachers, school administrators and other helping professionals learned these principles, they consistently reported unusually positive results with children, youth and adults in schools, mental health clinics, businesses, jails and community agencies. The principles *MGI* shares focus on individuals discovering their natural inner wisdom and innate mental health. This understanding is now gaining international recognition and respect. We can all be so grateful for the opportunity to explore the principles' profound life-changing message of hope.

Heartfelt thanks go to the team of volunteer dedicated professionals who assisted me in creating *MGI II*. Jane Tucker, who co-authored the **My Guide Inside** Learner Book II, wrote *Koa's Story* and *Jake's Story*, as well as the *Signal* and *Changing Your Mind* stories. I was inspired by Jeffery Timm's ideas for Wesley's and Amara's narratives and by Alberta Jacobs for Tanis' theme. Tom Tucker artfully produced the cover and this format and Jo Aucoin created our special owl graphic.

As author, school teacher and principal, Barb Aust, over forty years, saw the principles bring out the best in students and teachers. She and Kathy Marshall Emerson of the National Resilience Resource Center reviewed extensively and provided important links between the principles, curriculum guidelines, and sound research regarding education, resilience, and related fields. Kathy initially strongly encouraged me to undertake this curriculum and, behind the scenes assisted me extensively with *Learner Books* and in co-creating the *MGI Teacher Manuals*.

My husband Bob Campsall contributed insights and encouraged me every step of the way. Our son, Michael, created the accompanying website for *MGI*. For all children, youth and adult reviewers who offered their suggestions and reflections, and moved *MGI* along, many, many thanks!

–The Author

My Guide Inside® (Book II) Teacher's Manual

Overview of My Guide Inside Comprehensive Curriculum

About the Authors

Christa Campsall (right) has a 40+ year legacy teaching the principles shared in MGI. This has been the foundation of her work as a classroom teacher, learning services teacher in special education and school-based team chair. She has a BEd and DiplSpEd from University of British Columbia, and a MA from Royal Roads University. Along with MGI curriculum development, Christa facilitates professional development for educators in the global community.

Kathy Marshall Emerson (left), National Resilience Resource Center founding director, facilitates long-term school community principle–based training and systems change. Her free and globally available recorded webinar series, Educators Living in the Joy of Gratitude, features international veteran educators' outcomes of sharing the principles for as much as forty years in classrooms, school systems, and student services. She has a MA from the University of Southern California and is adjunct faculty at the University of Minnesota.

My Guide Inside is a three-part, comprehensive, Pre-K-12 story-based curriculum covering developmentally appropriate topics, in an ongoing process of learning that extends throughout the entire school career. As a teacher, you choose the level of *My Guide Inside* that is just right for your students in your particular school system: **Book I** (introduction, primary), **Book II** (continuation, intermediate), and **Book III** (advanced, secondary). This allows school leaders to chart a continuous instructional plan to share the Three Principles with students through the grades.

Objectives of *My Guide Inside* (Book II): The principles discussed in this learner book operate in all people, including every student. This *MGI* curriculum points the way to wholeness, happiness, creativity and well-being in all parts of life.
Therefore, *MGI* has these two globally appropriate academic goals to:
(1) Enhance Personal Well-being with an understanding of these principles, and
(2) Develop competencies in Communication, Thinking, and Personal and Social Awareness and Responsibility.
MGI accomplishes both goals by using stories, discussion and various written and creative activities, as the learning increases your students' competency in English Language Arts and several other areas.

Discovering their guide inside is key to learning, and it enhances children's ability to make decisions, navigate life, and build healthy relationships. Accessing this natural wisdom affects well-being, spiritual wellness, personal and social awareness and responsibility, and positive personal and cultural identity. Social and emotional learning, including self-determination, self-regulation, and self-efficacy, is also a natural outcome of greater awareness of one's own inner wisdom/"guide inside." See what kids think: watch the My Guide Inside Overview (5min) and Focus Group Experiences with My Guide Inside video of secondary student outcomes: 5min summary or full 27min interview myguideinside.com

This *MGI Teacher's Manual* accompanies **My Guide Inside** Learner Book II. The learner book, under separate title, offers a hopeful, simple way for learners to become aware of how they operate mentally from the inside-out. This understanding maximizes personal well-being and improves school climate, learner behavior and academic performance.

The *MGI Teacher's Manual* contains lesson plans, pre- and post-assessments, activities, evaluation scales and resources. We introduce universal principles making this curriculum for global use with all learners. In addition, we reference curriculum guidelines from Canada, United Kingdom, and United States.

- *MGI* meets selected requirements for *English Language Arts, Career Education, Health Education and Personal, Social, Health and Economic Education.*
- *MGI* supports inclusion and develops *Communication, Social and Emotional Learning, Personal Well-being Awareness, Social Awareness and Responsibility, and Thinking* competencies.

MGI Book II is appropriate for all learners in any intermediate classroom, older learners on a modified program, home learners, self-directed learners working independently, individual learners in counseling or personal coaching and in discussions with parents. Reading Level is "Easy to Read." Ideal age is 9-12, usually intermediate level. Most importantly this comprehensive curriculum offers a flexible framework to customize, adapt or modify to fit each teacher's understanding of the principles and the needs of students.

My Guide Inside® is available on myguideinside.com
Check the website for: E-books, MGI Online for schools, Video On Demand Classes, Training for Educators, Online Resources, Translations, and More…

Instructional Materials for Pre K – 12 Learners
myguideinside.com

My Guide Inside® Pre-K -12 Comprehensive Curriculum
Campsall, C. with Marshall Emerson, K. (2018). *My Guide Inside, Learner Book I.*
Campsall, C. with Marshall Emerson, K. (2018). *My Guide Inside, Teacher Manual, Book I.*
Campsall, C., Tucker, J. (2017). *My Guide Inside, Learner Book II.*
Campsall, C. with Marshall Emerson, K. (2017). *My Guide Inside, Teacher Manual, Book II.*

Campsall, C. with Marshall Emerson, K. (2017). *My Guide Inside, Learner Book III*.
Campsall, C., with Marshall Emerson, K. (2017). *My Guide Inside, Teacher Manual Book III*.

Picture Book
Campsall, C., Tucker, J. (2017). *Whooo ... has a Guide Inside?*

Supplemental Books for Parents and Educators
Marshall Emerson, K. (2020). *Parenting with Heart*. Amazon international markets.
Tucker, J. (2020). *Insights: Messages of Hope, Peace and Love*. Amazon international markets.

Video on Demand Classes and E-books:
Check the website for additional information, updates, and online resources. Included are Video On Demand classes that bring each chapter to life.

What Professionals Say About My Guide Inside

"This beautifully composed curriculum is a must for school principals, teachers, and teacher assistants. It points educators and their students towards a natural and inner state of well-being. All participants are given multiple opportunities to become learners in a state of joy and to access their common sense and innate wisdom in all areas of life. *My Guide Inside* is a holistic approach with the essence of our humanity at its core."

Dean Rees-Evans, MSc
Teacher, Researcher, Well-being Mentor, Macksville, New South Wales, AU

"I have been a teacher in underserved schools in Baltimore, Miami and the Bronx for over 12 years. By sharing the simple understanding that students are able to decide how they wish to experience life through their choices about thought, I have seen aggressive students become peacemakers, shy, self-conscious children become confident leaders, and the level of consciousness and empathy raised in an entire school. I am thrilled that this curriculum will be seen and experienced by so many! This understanding has the power to change education and the school experience on a global scale!"

Christina G. Puccio, MEd
MGI Video on Demand Discussant, Teacher, Mentor Teacher, PS 536, Bronx, NY, US

"Words fail my deepest desire to say 'Thank You' for the *My Guide Inside* materials. The knowledge they contain is a gift for every child."

Dr. Virgil Wood, Educator
Author In Love We Still Trust: Lessons We Learned from Martin Luther King Jr., and Sr.
Houston, TX, US

"*My Guide Inside* brings children and youth into contact with their own wisdom. Christa and Jane remind readers about the power of our thinking and support us to practice 'knowing' through listening. The beautiful tapestry of stories helps readers to 'think and see clearly.' This book is an extraordinary resource…a gift for us all."

Nia Williams, MA
Guidance Counselor, Gulf Islands, BC, CA

"I am so happy *My Guide Inside* will help many teachers and students find their inner wisdom. Their educational experience and personal lives will be enhanced."

Helen Neal-Ali
MGI Video On Demand Discussant, Facilitator, Author OK Forever: A book of hope
Tampa, FL, US

"Parents and teachers alike will find this a helpful resource as they work with children and youth to find the wisdom that lies inside each one of them, and to develop strategies for solving problems with the help of their own special guide."

Kelda Logan, MA
Principal, Salt Spring Island, BC, CA

"These authentic stories are simple, yet profound, and have the capacity to lead students to their Guide Inside."

Barb Aust, BEd, MEd
Principal, Education Consultant
Author The Essential Curriculum: 21 ideas for developing a positive and optimistic culture
Salt Spring Island, BC, CA

"As a headteacher (principal) for over thirty years, I have often witnessed first-hand the restless struggles many children and youth experience as they begin to feel comfortable in their own skin. Christa and Jane's straightforward, simple but profound curriculum helps teachers to point youth in a different direction, to our Guide Inside, our essence, our wisdom. I would recommend this guide to teachers as a powerful source of support. It helps us all remember who we really are … pure love."

Peter Anderson, Cert. Edn. Adv. Diploma (Cambridge)
Three Principles Facilitator, Headteacher Advisor, Essex, UK

My Guide Inside® Comprehensive Curriculum

well-being *communication* *resilience* *relationships*
responsibility *academic success* *happiness* *self-efficacy*

My Guide Inside (MGI) is designed to bring out the best in all students. A senior completing *My Guide Inside* classes wisely said…

"Mental wellness needs to be part of every school district's policies because if students are in a place where they do not feel they are capable to learn and don't have that emotional capacity to learn, school is not going to be successful."

For other My Guide Inside offerings, see
myguideinside.com

www.ingramcontent.com/pod-product-compliance
Lightning Source LLC
Chambersburg PA
CBHW042027150426
43198CB00002B/86